Can you spot the extra little frogs that are hiding in some of the pictures?

Author
Gill Marshall

Illustrator
Julie Pearce

I'll Just be a Tad

With special thanks to Bunty!

Tad was not feeling very happy.
"I'm not like other frogs," he said to himself.

Tad thought all other frogs lived in ponds and swamps, eating bugs and splashing around in cold mud.

Tad lived in a house and his favourite splash around was in the bath, with lots of bubbles.

And can you guess Tad's favourite food?

Tad wondered what it would be
like to be someone else.

While out walking, Tad saw Bizzy the honey bee, happily buzzing around, whizzing through the air without a care in the world.

"Wow," Tad said to Bizzy. "I wish I was a bee. I'd have fun flying."

"It is fun to fly," agreed Bizzy. "I'm working. I collect pollen from the flowers and then I take it home to make honey."

"Working," said Tad thoughtfully. "Where's your home?"

"Follow me," said Bizzy.

"This is called a hive. I have a big family and we all live together."

"OH!" Tad exclaimed. "Well, it was great to meet you all," and he hurried away.

"Phew," he thought, "I'm glad I'm not a bee. They don't have a soft bed to go home to every night."

As Tad walked on, he passed Jazz, dozing in the sun.

"What an easy life," Tad thought. "I could be a cat."

"Hello Jazz."

Jazz opened his eyes and stretched.

"Hello," he said, sleepily.

St-r-e-tch

"I'd like to be a cat," said Tad. "I could snooze in the sun all day."

"I also chase mice," said Jazz. "And I have to wash myself, like this."

"Oh!" exclaimed Tad. "I wash in the bath with lots of bubbles."

"I hate water," said Jazz.

"It's time for some fish now.
I have fish every day and
it's yummy.
Bye Tad."

As Jazz sauntered off Tad breathed a sigh of relief.

"Urgh, I'm glad I'm not a cat," he thought. "I wouldn't want fish every day."

Tad then saw Crystal galloping around her field.

"Gosh," thought Tad, waving to Crystal.
"She has fun. I could be a horse."

Crystal trotted over.

"Hi Crystal," said Tad. "If I was a horse, I could play with you."

"Nay-y-y, I'm not playing," said Crystal. "I'm exercising. I also eat this grass and sleep in a barn at night."

"OH!" exclaimed Tad. "Exercising, eating grass and sleeping in a barn."

"Yes," said Crystal. "There's plenty of hay and the spiders keep me company. I must carry on with my exercises."

Tad shivered as Crystal galloped away.

"Sleeping with spiders….I'm glad I'm not a horse," he thought.

Tad was thinking about his day when a voice interrupted.

"Oh hi Phoebe."

Phoebe sat down and started swinging her legs.

"Phoebe, I don't want to be a honey bee, cat or horse. I've decided, I'll just be a Tad," said Tad.

"That's a relief Tad," Phoebe said, pointing to his long legs. "You wouldn't be able to do your special jump."

"You're right," Tad said, running to the pond.

Tad squatted down as low as he could.
As he did, he made a funny beeping noise,
sounding a bit like a robot.

"Take aim," he said, raising his arms and leaning forward. "Adjust for wind speed and direction, beeeep beeeeep and.......Peeeowwwww!"

Tad leapt high into the air and easily jumped over the pond.

"Amazing! I wish I could do that," croaked a frog, leaping into the water.

"That was so cool Tad," said Phoebe.

Tad looked at his long legs and smiled.

That evening, Tad chuckled as he thought about his adventures.

"I'm glad I'm me," he said to himself.

Tad was a happy frog again.

Did you spot the hidden frogs?

Tad's Frog Facts

I have discovered there are over 4,800 species of frog and they don't all live in swamps and ponds. Here are some of my favourites:

The Mossy Frog pretends to be a moss-covered rock. It has large, sticky pads on its toes and belly, and it curls into a ball when danger is near.

The Desert Rain Frog buries itself in the sand and has a high-pitched squeak, often called its war cry.

The Indian Bullfrog can jump on the water surface just as it would jump on land!

The Blue Poison Dart Frog and Yellow-Banded Poison Dart Frog have loud calls and can give out poisons through their skin to protect them from being eaten by larger animals.

My favourite is the Wallace Flying Frog that lives mainly in trees. It has long, webbed toes that act like a parachute when it jumps.

Printed in Great Britain
by Amazon

67945759R00017